MW00876503

DUMB BUNNY
THE GREAT

Dumb Bunny the Great

Svevo Brooks

Illustrated by Zoe Mendez

LUMINARE PRESS

WWW.LUMINAREPRESS.COM

Luminare Press
442 Charnelton St.
Eugene, OR 97401
www.luminarepress.com

LCCN: 2021915840
ISBN: 978-1-64388-695-4

TO ALL BUNNIES
GREAT AND SMALL

The two-leggeds witnessed the birth. Crouched behind a downed log, they watched newborn cottontails jostle to get at the doe's milk. A cottontail buck, ears turning, nose quivering, scanned earth and sky for predators.

"Eight," the woman's long, braided hair was tied with a strip of beaded buckskin. "Sixteen ears, thirty-two paws."

"Seven," said the man. "The puny one will never survive. They push him away and won't let him nurse."

"Mother Nature will decide," said the woman.

The man notched an arrow in the bow and sited the cottontail buck along the shaft.

The woman grabbed his arm to keep him from shooting. "We'll eat acorn bread and camas," she said.

The man removed the arrow and put the bow on the ground. "The runt will have a father," he said.

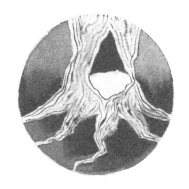

CHAPTER 1

Horace was his name. Horace Cottontail.

The kits called him Runt.

"You, Runt—outta the way!"

"Pull Runt's tail—if you can find it!"

"Runt, Runt, watch him grunt!"

Horace was small, weak, and shy. Instead of nursing with his cottontail brothers and sisters he waited until they were done and nursed alone. Instead of sleeping with the kits in a big, warm pile, he slept by himself. When the kits romped in the Great Meadow he stayed in the warren with his mother.

Worried Horace was too frail to survive, his father made an elixir from devil's club and usnea, plants reputed to impart strength. The elixir, fermented in the hollow bole of an oak tree, had an astonishing effect. After one month, Horace was bigger than his brothers and sisters. After two months he was bigger than his father. By the midsummer blackberry moon he was twice the size of any cottontail in the warren. His eyes were like oak galls, his ears the size of cedar boughs. His paws resembled beaver pads.

Horace was clumsy. Instead of hopping gracefully, he moved with a lumbering gait. He tripped over his paws. When he tried to bound, he somersaulted and landed in a heap. He broke tunnel walls, knocked over furniture, and frightened the other kits.

Not only was Horace slow-footed, he also was slow-witted. Instead of talking, he repeated what had just been said, grunted, rolled his eyes, flipped his tail, and flopped his ears. He also had a curious and remarkable ability—he said words backward. Ecaroh, he called himself. Ecaroh Liatnottoc.

The kits teased Horace. They called him Dumb Bunny. They made jokes about his long ears and huge paws. They snuck up behind him and pulled his tail. They poked him with sticks and threw clumps of dirt at him. Horace never complained or hit back. He just sat on his haunches with a curious, bemused smile.

Horace's father taught the kits survival skills. He described cottontail enemies—what they looked like, how they smelled, stalked, and hunted. He imitated wolverine cries and scratched coyote tracks in the dirt. He took the kits on reconnaissance missions and pointed out signs of danger—tufts of fur, scents, broken twigs, bent grass, chewed bones. He taught the kits to sit as still as a stone and showed them the root hollow, a secret hiding place at the base of the Great Pine.

While the other kits looked at possum tracks and coyote droppings, Horace daydreamed and wandered. He stared at worms and bugs, watched spiders weave webs, and ants carry eggs and bits of grass. He sniffed flowers, licked drops of dew, and stared at the sky. Told to hide or dive into a hole, he put his paws over his eyes.

Cottontail elders, worried Horace would attract predators and endanger the clan, wanted to banish him from the warren.

Horace's father reassured the elders. "I'll watch him constantly," he promised. "Horace will never be out of my sight."

Horace's mother kissed her son a thousand times and made him a thistledown bed.

CHAPTER 2

Snow came the night of the winter moon. Four nights and four days flakes tumbled from Mother Nature's weather pouch, weaving a thick, white quilt over the Great Meadow. Bucks cleaned tunnels and does spun fur. Kits—except Horace, who stayed in the warren with his mother—played in the snow. They made snow bunnies, played snow tag, and had snowball fights. They built a castle with secret tunnels, a dungeon, and a cave for hiding treasure. The kits' favorite game was leap-bunny; shouting gleefully, they jumped off a downed log and dove into a snowbank.

The kits were playing leap-bunny when one of them said, "Let's get Dumb Bunny. He's huge. His shoulders are as wide as a tree. It will be like jumping off a mountain!"

"Horace has never seen snow," Amanda Cottontail shook her ears when the kits came to the warren home. "He might get cold. He might get lost. He might…"

"Please let Horace play," begged the kits. "Snow's magic."

"Don't worry, my dear," Reginald Cottontail put a gentle paw on his wife's shoulder. "I'll watch Horace the whole time.

It will do him good. He's never seen snow. He's never played with the kits before."

"Don't let him wander," Amanda Cottontail cautioned. "I want all our precious children to know the wonders of the Great Meadow."

FRESH, POWDERY SNOW CAST A LUMINOUS GLOW OVER THE Great Meadow. Cottonwood trees, barren for two moons, wore elegant white gowns. Teasel stalks sported jaunty white hats. Ferns bowed low. Whiteness dusted every clump of dirt and blade of grass.

Reginald Cottontail watched proudly as his son played with the other kits. Eyes glistening, nostrils quivering, Horace flicked his tongue in and out, catching snowflakes. When a flake landed on his nose he laughed and shook his head from side to side.

The kits jumped from the downed log, bounced off Horace's shoulders, and catapulted into the snowbank. Horace stood perfectly still. Even when a paw cuffed his ear, he didn't move a whisker.

"Bravo!" the kits clapped their tiny paws. "Bravo for Dumb Bunny the Great!"

Horace grunted happily. His eyes glistened. His tail swished from side to side. He clapped his massive paws. Never had he heard such beautiful words. He wasn't Dumb Bunny anymore, he was Dumb Bunny the Great!

Warning cries interrupted the revelry. "Aiee!" cawed ravens from the branches of the Great Pine. "Aiee! Aiee!"

"Danger!" Reginald Cottontail drummed his hind legs on the snow. "Freeze!"

The kits became statues, their bodies gray and brown stones. The Great Pine sighed. Wind rustled dried mugwort stalks.

"Take cover!" Reginald Cottontail drummed louder. "Back to the warren!"

The kits ran pell-mell to the blackberry thicket. Pushing and shoving, they crawled under brambles and dove into the tunnel.

Reginald Cottontail followed the kits and pulled brush over the tunnel entrance. "Where's Horace?" He looked anxiously from bunny to bunny.

"Maybe he went home," said one trembling kit.

"Maybe he stayed at the log," said another.

"Maybe he's catching snowflakes," suggested a third.

Reginald Cottontail dashed through the maze of tunnels. "Have you seen Horace?" He looked anxiously at his wife. "He's not with the other kits."

"How could you?" Amanda Cottontail dropped the tufts of fur she was spinning. "Go find him! Go find my precious son!"

An ominous silence hung over the Great Meadow. Birds had stopped singing. Trees had stopped sighing. Even the wind was mute.

Ears turning, nose quivering, Reginald Cottontail made his way to the downed log. He looked below the log where Horace had stood and in the brush surrounding the log. Fresh snow covered everything. There were no paw prints or scents, nothing to indicate the kits had been there.

Fear gripped Reginald Cottontail as he searched for his son. He looked in culverts and gullies, behind rocks and mounds of snow. He went to the Great Pine and looked in the root hollow. He searched the banks of the Lesser Stream and the edges of the Ancient Bog. He found no clues—no tracks, scents, scat, tufts of fur, or paw marks.

The same snow that minutes before had made Horace so happy now covered any trace of his fate.

CHAPTER 3

Silently, wings pressed against its bones, the owl dropped from the sky and drove its talons into Horace's flanks. Yellow eyes glowing with excitement, the owl rose into the darkness until the downed log, the blackberry thicket, and the Great Pine—the boundaries of Horace's world—disappeared from sight.

Mother Nature made Horace quiet and gentle. He was more like a butterfly than a rabbit. Noise frightened him. He moved slowly, admiring ants and spiderwebs, licking dewdrops. Instead of romping and playing, he sniffed flowers and stared at clouds.

Pain changed Horace. He kicked and squirmed, flapped his ears, threw his massive head from side to side. When pain from the owl's talons became so great that his stomach heaved and tears clouded his eyes, he screamed—a plaintive wail that sent creatures below scurrying for cover.

The owl had caught mice, voles, possums, snakes, even a small fox. But never had it carried a creature as big and heavy as Horace. The more Horace struggled, the more the owl struggled to hold him. Instead of flying straight across the Great Meadow, it lurched and weaved. Instead of flying above the Lesser Stream, it barely skimmed the water. When the owl reached the Great Forest, it careened recklessly between the trees.

The vicelike talon grip loosened. The pain wasn't as sharp. It became easier to breathe. Slowly, like waking from a nightmare, things became visible again—trees, falling snow, patches of earth.

Horace plummeted from the sky and crashed through a snowbank.

FURIOUS AT LOSING ITS PREY, THE OWL BEAT ITS WINGS SO fast they sounded like thunder. It screamed, dove down, and clawed at the snow and brush through which Horace had plunged. Each time the owl attacked, Horace crouched low and put his paws over his eyes. At daybreak, the owl made one last futile dive. Glaring at the impenetrable snowbank, it left the Great Forest, crossed the Lesser Stream, and flew back to the Great Meadow.

Horace cowered beneath the snowbank. His body trembled. Blood reddened his white and gray fur. When the owl scent was gone, he licked his wounds. His nose, chin, and lips were cut. Both ears were bleeding. Blood oozed from talon wounds in his flanks.

Rhythmic licking calmed Horace. He stopped shaking. His eyes stopped wandering. His stomach quit churning. When the bleeding slowed, he pushed back snow and stretched out. Putting his head on his paws, he slept.

Horace had two dreams.

In the first dream, kits were bouncing off his shoulders. "Dumb Bunny! Dumb Bunny!" they shouted. "The Great! The Great!" Horace added after each shout.

In the second dream, Horace was in the warren, sleeping on his thistledown bed. Father brought him clover and berries. Mother kissed him a thousand times and told him not to cry.

WHEN HORACE AWOKE HE WAS SURPRISED TO DISCOVER
he wasn't sleeping in a warm thistledown bed but in a cold, damp
snow cave. Mother wasn't there to kiss him. Father wasn't there to
bring him food. He was alone. Alone and hungry. His stomach felt
hollow, his head dizzy. Stiff, sore, and tired, he wanted to laze and
keep sleeping. But hunger wouldn't let him rest. He had to move.
He had to find food.

Horace's huge paws were well suited for digging. He tunneled
through snow until he came to a boulder. He dug under and
around the boulder but it was always there, blocking his way. He
leaned on the boulder and licked his wounds. A thin beam of
moonlight breached the snow and flickered on a giant paw. Mesmerized by the flickering light, he tunneled up, broke through
frozen turf, and poked his head into the night.

Snow had stopped falling. Big trees hid most of the sky.
Horace sniffed the wind and rotated his ears. Satisfied the owl
was gone, he hopped to a tree, swiped snow from a bough, and
took a bite of the greenery. He spit over and over but the bitter
taste wouldn't leave his mouth.

Cedar branches drooped low and disappeared under the snow.
Horace circled until he found an opening. Flattening out on his belly,
he wriggled under snow-covered boughs. Beneath the tree, protected
from wind and cold, the air was still. Instead of deep snow there
were scattered patches. Grass grew thickly around the cedar's trunk.

Horace ate fast, barely swallowing one bite of grass before
snatching another. It wasn't sweet, like grass in the Great Meadow,
but it slaked his hunger. When his stomach was full, he looked
around for a place to rest. At the base of the cedar was a hollow
bole. Inside the bole was a pile of dry moss. He pushed the moss
around until it fit the shape of his body. Then he stretched out,
closed his eyes, and slept.

Until an acorn hit him on the head.

CHAPTER 4

"Out!" Flashing green eyes glared from the bole opening. "Scram! Scoot! Vamoose! *Foutez le camp!* Beat it!"

The owner of the flashing green eyes was a squirrel. He had a gray nose, gray eyes, and a gray tail. His tail was longer than his body. A thin black stripe ran up his back.

"You're trespassing!" The squirrel shook an angry paw. "Explain yourself. And be quick about it. There are laws against this kind of thing. And creatures that enforce them!"

"Please and sorry," Horace couldn't remember which word came first. "Sorry and please."

"Please and sorry?" snapped the squirrel. "That's a fine excuse. I suppose you walk in wherever you please—right into a private domicile. And disturb a creature's elegant and expensive furnishings." He pointed at the flattened moss. "Surely you can distinguish public from private property. Does this look like an abandoned hovel? I worked moons building this place. Moons! For all I know you've eaten my acorns. Out of the way so I can examine the larder."

Horace stood up. His head hit the top of the hollow bole.

"Zounds!" Seeing how big Horace was, the squirrel backed away fast. "Double-zounds!"

"Sdnuoz," Horace said. "Elbuod-sdnuoz."

"Lummox!" The squirrel was careful to keep his distance. "Gargantuan!"

"Cottontail," Horace flipped his tail. He didn't know what a lummox or gargantuan was.

"Cottontail my paw!" The squirrel eyed Horace suspiciously. "I've seen plenty of them in my day. Plenty. Believe me, they aren't half as big as you. Most likely you're some kind of mutated lagomorph."

Horace grunted and shook his ears. Lagomorph sounded like a bad thing to be.

"Lagomorphs, for your information," said the squirrel, "are creatures with sharp front teeth. Cottontails, hares, and picas are lagomorphs. For lack of a more precise definition of what you are, and giving you the benefit of considerable doubt, I shall consider you a lagomorph."

Horace yawned. Before the acorn hit him he'd been sleeping deeply.

"I knew it!" Seeing Horace's teeth, the squirrel gasped. "A rapacious creature—eater!"

"Clover," Horace said.

"Flesh!"

"Milkweed," Horace said.

"With incisors like a bobcat!"

"Dandelion," Horace said.

"Bones and gristle!"

Horace took a step toward the bole opening.

"Just kidding," the squirrel backed up fast. "No offense intended."

Horace followed the squirrel outside the bole. "Much obliged," he pointed at the grass and rubbed his stomach. "Obliged much."

"Take all you want," the squirrel waved a dismissive paw. "Stuff's a nuisance. Attracts nothing but pests and pestilence."

"Pestilence and pests," Horace said. "Pests and pestilence."

"Don't mention it," said the squirrel. "Especially to strangers. Just make sure you come alone. But don't touch the acorns. Acorns are definitely not in the public domain."

"Don't mention it," Horace said. "Definitely not in the public domain."

"Must you repeat everything I say?" said the squirrel irritably. "If I want to listen to myself talk, I'll talk to myself. By the way," he flipped his tail, "Sylvester's the name. Everybody around here knows me. Everybody friendly, that is."

"Ecaroh," Horace patted the top of his head the way Father taught him. "Ecaroh Liatnottoc."

"What did you call me?!"

"Horace Cottontail," he patted his head again.

"Horace? What an appellation! I once knew a badger named Boris. Mean old cuss. Chewed everything in sight—until he chewed around a wolverine den one night. Where do you come from? Not around here, that's for sure. I've never seen one like you. Never!"

Horace lifted a paw and pointed at the sky.

"Ha!" The squirrel rolled his eyes. "And now I suppose you're going to tell me you can fly. Using those skunk cabbage ears for wings. I wasn't born yesterday. Or the day before!"

Horace hopped to where the boughs of the cedar disappeared beneath the snow. Crouching low, he ducked under the branches and wriggled through to the other side.

Sylvester waited until all he could see was white fluff on the tip of Horace's tail. Then he hit him on the rump with a snowball.

"And he calls himself a cottontail!" muttered the squirrel.

CHAPTER 5

Horace stumbled through the falling snow.

Three nights had passed since he fell from the sky. Three cold, lonely, hungry nights. Now he was going home. Back to Mother and Father. Back to the warren and his thistledown bed. No more sleeping in a cold, damp snow cave. No more eating bark, bitter boughs, and dried up grass. When he was thirsty, he ate snow. When he felt pain and soreness, he licked his wounds. As he traveled he sniffed the wind, turned his ears, and scanned the sky for the owl.

Celestial cottontails—cottontails who died and went to live in the sky—were Horace's guides. They winked at him. They showed him which trails to take, which to avoid. Horace's grandparents and great-grandparents were celestial cottontails. So was Uncle Nettle, killed by a wolverine. Mother said that when Uncle Nettle went to live in the sky the moon had a piece missing—a bite from the wolverine's teeth.

The sky changed. It was dark, then light, then dark again. Horace preferred darkness. He could see better. Smells were keener. Celestial cottontails were brighter and easier to follow. The darkness teemed with sounds: trees groaned, wind sighed, leaves rustled. The call of a lone night bird, faint and distant, beckoned Horace. "This way. This way, Ecaroh," the bird seemed to say. "I will lead you home."

Horace made a discovery—another cottontail was traveling on the same path. He recognized the familiar smell. The tracks matched his own, as did the tufts of brown fur clinging to brambles.

Hoping to overtake the cottontail and travel with it back to the warren, Horace walked faster. But no matter how fast he walked, the mysterious traveler was always gone. At first there was just one set of prints in the snow but the longer he traveled, the more prints he saw. The path became as well beaten as a deer run.

Light nibbled steadily at darkness. Horace's shadow grew dimmer. Morning birds began to sing; trills, tweets, chirps, and warbles announced the wakening sun. Familiar landmarks—bushes, trees, gullies, mounds of snow, broken limbs, snapped branches—greeted him at every turn. *I'm almost home*, Horace thought with mounting excitement. *A few more steps and I'll see the Great Pine, the blackberry thicket, and the warren. Mother and Father will hug me. I'll play leap bunny with the kits and tell them about flying through the sky. They'll cheer and cry, "Dumb Bunny the Great!"*

The tracks led to a snowbank. Beneath the snowbank was a tunnel and a flattened place that perfectly fit the contours of his body. Exhausted from hours of walking, he put his head between his paws and fell into a deep sleep.

When Horace awoke, he made a startling discovery. He wasn't in his thistledown bed. He wasn't in the warm, dry warren with Mother, Father, and the kits. He'd traveled the entire night and ended up back where he started—under the cold, damp snowbank where he'd taken refuge from the owl.

CHAPTER 6

"Great gophers!" Sylvester, perched on a cedar limb, shook a paw at Horace. "Have you no shame, fellow? Bad enough to throw rubbish around for everyone to see, but to throw it right on my doorstep. Surely you can find better things to do with those clodhopper paws."

Horace stared at his feet. "Devil's clubs," the kits called his paws. Devil's club was the spiky plant Father put in the elixir.

"Am I making myself clear?" Sylvester pointed at the mound of dirt outside the hole. "Move it! Get that mess out of my sight!"

Horace looked back and forth between the mound and the angry squirrel. Then he turned and kicked dirt back into the hole.

"Not *in* the hole for beaver-sake!" Sylvester slapped the side of his head with his tail. "*Away* from it! Break up those clumps. Spread the dirt around. Wipe out your paw prints. Surely you've heard of such things. Last night, when you followed yourself in circles, you left enough tracks for a lagomorph army. A blind, senile fox could follow a trail like that! Fortunately, it snowed and covered your gaucheries. Gaucheries, by the way, is not a compliment. It's the French way of saying you blundered."

Horace pulled a briar from his tail. He pulled so hard he tumbled backward into the snow.

"Stop dawdling!" Sylvester stared nervously at the dried blood on Horace's stomach. "Get to work! The only thing worse than a lazy creature is two lazy creatures!"

Horace did everything Sylvester told him. He spread the mound of dirt. He scattered twigs, boughs, and leaves over the dirt. He kicked fresh snow on top of the dirt. When he finished, the area around the hole looked just like any other part of the Great Forest.

"Marvelous! Stupendous!" Sylvester clapped his paws together. "We make some team, eh, Horace? I can see it now. S & H Construction. Excavation. Demolition. Renovation. Brain and brawn—what a combination. We'll make a fortune. An absolute fortune!"

"Brain and brawn," Horace stared wide-eyed at the chattering squirrel. "What a combination."

"Never mind," Sylvester drummed his tail on a limb. "We'll draw up a contract later. Better yet, we'll keep the whole plan secret. I know this place like the tips of my whiskers. And all the villainous creatures that prowl it. They're not to be trusted—any of them! I had a friend once, an old mole. The most generous and amiable fellow you can imagine. One winter it got bitterly cold. Trees cracked. The Lesser Stream froze. There wasn't an acorn between here and the Great Sand Mountain. The mole got hungrier and more desperate. You could see it in his eyes—they were wild and crazed. The old mole had a mate, a lovely sow who had borne him dozens of children. She was hungry and weak but never complained. One day the old mole went out looking for food. He found a cache hidden inside a hollow log. Roots, nuts, seeds, dried berries—you name it. He ate himself silly. Then he slept, got up, and ate himself silly again. The bugger stayed right there, eating and sleeping the whole winter. He never went back to his mate, never returned home. All that food, every last morsel, he hoarded for himself. The sow died of starvation."

Horace had heard stories about moles. Father said moles dug holes in warren tunnels and stole food from the storehouse. Mother said moles had beautiful whiskers. The kits said moles smelled like skunk cabbage and their burps started fires. The death of the sow made Horace sad.

"Where was I?" Sylvester continued. "Oh yes, trust and neighborhood decorum. They're not to be trusted—any of them. Even the friendliest creatures, ones that greet you amiably every day, think nothing of stealing your food. Or even your pelt! That's why I have no intention of mentioning your arrival. As far as I'm concerned, you're just an itinerant creature who happens to be passing through. If anyone asks, I'll say that and nothing more. I don't know who you are, where you came from, or where you're headed. Do you get the gist of what I'm saying? Keep your ears tuned to trouble and your paws off other creatures' acorns. If you follow that simple advice, you'll live to see another sunrise."

"Sunrise," Horace grunted. "Esirnus."

"Let's not stand here and be maudlin all night!" Sylvester flew from the cedar to the ground. "What's done is done. The past, however despicable, is gone. The future, however alluring, is mysterious and unknown. Only one thing matters—survival. Make haste. Scamper into your hole and do whatever it is lagomorphs do in their subterranean compounds. As for me, I must return to my domicile and get my affairs in order. Inclement weather is approaching. I can feel it in my spleen. You, of course, living beneath the earth, are largely unaffected by Mother Nature's tumultuous moods."

"Mother Nature," Horace remembered Mother's voice, how it rose excitedly as she told a bedtime story about Mother Nature, "made the sky and the Great Pine."

"Perhaps the sky," Sylvester said, "but the Great Pine, definitely not. Mother Nature would never do such shabby work. That tree is a widow-maker. You look at a limb the wrong way and it snaps off. You breathe on a pine cone and it whacks you on the head. The Great Pine—the name alone is a fabrication—has cost me a small fortune. A stoat with dubious intentions runs a gambling establishment. Every year there's a lottery on whether the Great Pine will survive the winter. I've lost enough acorns to fill a cave!"

"Great garrulous gophers!" Sylvester ran over and looked down the hole. "This shaft goes straight down. A regular drain hole. The first thaw will fill it up like a lake. I've never seen such excavation. Never! Don't just stand there—do something! Put in bends and curves. Taper the sides—so they're not so steep. Dig drainage ditches. Get to work! *Au travail*!"

Horace's ears twitched. Somersaulting twice, he dove into the hole. Sylvester covered the opening with brush and fresh snow. Holding a cedar bough in his teeth, he swept the snow clear of tracks.

"That mole I told you about," Sylvester shouted through the snow and brush, "the one who abandoned his wife and gorged himself while she starved, died of his own gluttony. He ate himself to death. Every time I pass his grave I spit three times!"

CHAPTER 7

orace was hungry all the time. Even after eating he was
hungry. He couldn't find enough forage, and what little
he did find was dry and tasteless. Roots were shriveled,
boughs caked with ice, seeds half-eaten by insects. Grass under
the cedar was drier and harder to chew.

I was never hungry in the warren, Horace thought. *Father brought
me sweet meadow grass. Mother took me to a storehouse filled with
roots and seeds and berries. Are Mother and Father looking for me?
What if they think I live in the sky? When Uncle Nettle got killed by a
wolverine, the whole clan circled the Great Pine and wailed.*

To console himself, Horace made things out of snow. He made
clover and milk thistle—his favorite greens. He made Mother and
Father, carefully forming Mother's plump cheeks and Father's
long tail. When he was hungry he nibbled snow-clover and
snow-milk thistle. When he was lonely he talked to Snow-Mother
and Snow-Father. He told them about the owl and the terrifying
journey across the sky. He told them about the Great Forest and
the snow cave and begged them to take him home.

DESPERATE FOR FOOD, HORACE WENT TO THE CEDAR, crawled under the drooping boughs, and nibbled the withered grass. Each bite had to be chewed over and over before it could be swallowed. He was chewing listlessly when a strange smell reached his nostrils. His tail twitched. His fur stiffened. Slowly, cautiously, he rotated his ears and turned his head.

Two smoldering red eyes glared at him from the hollow bole. Small and close together, the eyes were sunk deep inside the creature's head. Instead of staying in one place, the eyes darted from side to side.

"Ecaroh," Horace patted the top of his head. "Ecaroh Liatnottoc."

The creature dropped out of the bole. It had a long, thin body, black fur, and a stiff black tail. Its face, long and gaunt, had just enough room for a pointy nose, thin lips, and thin pink ears. Its chin was covered with bristly black whiskers. The smoldering red eyes darted and flashed.

"Brain and brawn," Horace said. "We'll make a fortune. An absolute fortune."

The creature raised a hooked claw.

"Take all you want," Horace pointed at the grass at the base of the cedar. "Stuff's a nuisance. Attracts nothing but pests and pestilence."

The creature snarled and took a step back. Then two steps back, and three. It stared at the dried blood on Horace's ears and the scars on his flanks. It stared at his huge paws and massive body. Never had it seen a rabbit so big. Or so bold. Rabbits were meek. They didn't fight; they cowered and ran. This one, covered with battle scars, wasn't afraid.

"But don't touch the acorns," Horace flipped his tail the way Sylvester did. "Acorns are definitely not in the public domain. Another thing. When you make a mess, clean it up. Neighborhood decorum. And when you leave, cover your tracks. If you do all that you'll live to see another day."

Hissing and baring its razor-sharp teeth, the creature crept away from the hollow bole. Instead of eating the grass Horace offered, it crawled under the cedar boughs and ran into the forest.

CHAPTER 8

"Great gnats!" Sylvester bounced up and down on a cedar limb. "Even during the Mighty Flood I never witnessed such valor. Imagine a weasel, a base, good-for-nothing thief of a weasel, slinking off like that. Without an acorn or a piece of flesh! I saw it all," he clapped his paws and swooshed his tail. "The way you feigned indifference. The way you measured your opponent, even as he advanced. The way you dispatched him—as though he was a harmless stump!"

"Without an acorn," Horace looked up at the chattering squirrel, "or a piece of flesh."

"Weasels," Sylvester ran a paw across his throat, "are assassins. Nothing more, nothing less. Other creatures, it is true, also kill. They have to, to survive. Weasels, on the other paw, kill simply for entertainment. They don't even eat their poor victims. Did you know the weasel was a mistake? Mother Nature thought she was making a boar, a creature that roots around in the earth. Little did she know she was creating a monster!"

Horace licked his whiskers. When he lived in the warren he

sometimes found bits of food hidden in the bristles. Now he found nothing—not even a crumb.

"Let's talk of more pleasant things," Sylvester pointed at the sky. "Like the weather. And the price of acorns. And the vast economic potential of S & H Construction. I hope you don't mind that S comes before H. My name, for better or worse, is known in the Great Forest. You, on the other paw, are a newcomer, an immigrant. Not that you are undeserving of accolades and recognition. Still, business is business, and if we are to make a success of this partnership we must be astute and put our best paws forward.

"Don't be shy. Eat heartily my pugilistic friend. Pugilistic, by the way, is a compliment. It means you know how to fight. It means you know how to defend both honor and turf. If I had a thousand meadows of grass I would give you exclusive foraging privileges. It's yours—every clump, every blade of greenery that embellishes my domain. It's the least I can do after you drove off that villainous weasel and saved my cache of nuts."

"Lesaew," said Horace, remembering the hollow eyes and whiskery chin of the sharp-nosed creature, "was hungry."

"Hungry for your flesh!" Sylvester frowned as Horace chewed listlessly on a clump of dried grass. "Look at you. Your cheeks are hollow as empty acorns. And your fur looks like it was caught in a teasel patch. Don't be ashamed. Hunger is a common affliction. I, fortunately, have never experienced it. I have twenty winters' worth of food stashed away and so many caches I can't remember where they are. I come by hoarding naturally. My parents were great hoarders, and my grandparents as well. Hoarding is a point of honor in the squirrel clan. How did you say you got here?"

"Owl," Horace licked his wounds and pointed at the sky.

"Weasels, wolverines, ferrets, foxes!" Sylvester scowled. "What a treacherous world we inhabit. How many times have friends disappeared before my very whiskers? How many times have I seen gentle, harmless creatures slaughtered by cruel, avaricious predators? That's why I feel compelled to help you. We may meet again. Then again, we may not. Winter is long and perilous. I like you, Horace, and hope you will live to see the spring. Ah, spring! What a glorious time. Fresh tender shoots to nourish the body. Radiant wildflowers to nourish the soul. The sparkle of dewdrops glistening in the morning sun...."

As Sylvester spoke, it started to snow. Snow dusted his coat and the limb on which he was perched. A solitary flake, a perfectly formed hexagon of glistening whiteness, landed on the tip of Horace's nose.

"Mother Nature," Sylvester scooped up a pawful of snow, "has an exclusive and proprietary patent on the snowflake. Her manufacturing factory, I'm told, is so secretive that even the employees don't know where it is. Unlike excavation, demolition, and renovation—the foundations of our new enterprise—snowflake production is a seasonal business. In summer, when there is a shortage of raw material, Mother Nature converts the factory to the production of beeswax, a product made with the same six-sided design as the snowflake."

Horace stared dreamily at the chattering squirrel. Like gusts of wind, Sylvester's words took him on long, beautiful journeys to places he'd never been.

CHAPTER 9

"Make haste!"

Tail billowing, Sylvester flew to the ground and landed at Horace's feet. "A blizzard's on the way. I can feel it in my spleen. Go back to your subterranean dwelling and make room for the acorns. Dig. Excavate. Make a storehouse—a place to keep provisions. Don't worry—you're doing me a favor. Now that that thieving weasel knows about my cache he'll be back to squander it. I'd rather see the nuts rot. Or even give them to my competitors!"

Horace tumbled into the tunnel and started digging. He worked fast, kicking load after load of dirt through the tunnel and out the entrance. Sylvester stood outside, shouting suggestions and instructions.

"Peel back the dirt slowly, layer by layer—like you were looking for buried treasure. Leave plenty of roots—they prevent cave-ins. Don't remove big rocks—it's fast but ultimately disastrous. Make the storehouse cavernous—twice as big as your imagination. We'll line it with cedar boughs. Cedar will give the acorns an agreeable flavor. You do like acorns, don't you? How could anyone *not* like them!"

Horace did everything Sylvester told him. He threw out dirt, used mud and twigs to shore up the walls, packed snow in cracks. He also dug a hole at the back of the tunnel —"a place to hide during emergencies, catastrophes, disasters, and general malfeasance," Sylvester said. "By malfeasance I refer to the boorish behavior of creatures with long, sharp teeth and lethal claws. Enough said."

"Marvelous, Horace, marvelous!" Sylvester dropped into the tunnel and ran his paws over the walls. "You're like a gopher. I don't mean you have the disposition or intelligence of a gopher. Gophers are—how shall I say it?—rather coarse. What I mean is, you and gophers share a certain predilection for digging. While you're at it, make another exit hole. You can never have too many escape hatches. Never! You won't be coming out that often—not if my information is correct. I took the liberty of speaking to a family of hares. After hearing my description of you, they said you definitely weren't a hare. They also said you definitely weren't a cottontail. With that I concur. Still, they did say that if you were a cottontail, which was highly unlikely, you wouldn't be in the Great Forest. Mother Nature would never allow it. That's why she made the Lesser Stream—to separate cottontails and hares and keep them from killing each other."

Horace had heard stories about hares. The kits called hares names and drew lewd pictures of them in the dirt. Father said hares were relatives but because they were wild and ill-mannered, Mother Nature had banished them from the Great Meadow.

"Here, try one of these," Sylvester pulled an acorn from his jaw and handed it to Horace. "Not the shell, the nut! What did I tell you? Delicious, aren't they? Wait until you see what they do for your vitality. You'll have the strength of a cougar!"

Horace chewed listlessly on the acorn. Like cedar boughs and withered grass, it was dry and bitter.

"Eat, eat," Sylvester took another acorn from his jaw, cracked it open, and handed the nut to Horace. "You need sustenance after doing all that work. Now that the storehouse is finished, Gravity will make the delivery."

"Gravity?" Horace grunted. "Ytivarg?"

"What! You mean you don't know Gravity? I thought everybody knew him. Gravity brings rain down and keeps rocks from flying up. Gravity keeps the moon from tumbling from the sky. Gravity keeps the sun from staying up night and day. Without Gravity we'd all be...never mind. You'll meet him soon enough. Here—have one more acorn. It will do you good."

Sylvester came back carrying cedar boughs in his mouth. "Fine. A fine piece of work," he dropped the boughs and sniffed the storehouse walls. "A little rough here and there but adequate under the circumstances." After that, he brought seventeen loads of cedar boughs and five loads of cedar bark. After each load he scratched a mark on the tunnel wall.

"It's time you met Gravity," Sylvester dropped the last load of bark, brushed dirt from his coat, and paced back and forth around the storehouse. "Gravity is a prodigious worker. He can also be boisterous and noisy. Catch the acorns as he pitches them to you. Lay them on the boughs. One caveat—make sure the acorns don't touch. Acorns that touch go rancid. Rancid acorns are worse than useless. When one row is full of acorns cover it with cedar boughs and start a new row.

"Yikes!" Sylvester pinched his nose. "This place smells mustier than a rotting skunk! Why live underground when a tree house affords fresh air and a magnificent view? What's that?" He pointed at a mound of snow at the side of the tunnel. "Why it looks like a lagomorph. A lagomorph sculpted of snow. And there's another one right beside it. Did you make these?"

"Mother," Horace's ears drooped. "Father."

"They're beautiful," Sylvester walked around the sculptures. "Not just beautiful, exquisite. You're an artisan, Horace. A true *artiste*."

Horace picked up a pawful of snow and patched a divot on Snow-Mother's arm. Then he hugged her.

"Poor boy," Sylvester laid a gentle paw on Horace's shoulder. "You're lonely. I can see it in your posture, the sadness in your eyes. Loneliness is a terrible affliction. Worse than hunger. Worse even than thirst. Never mind. Let's not be maudlin. To work. *Au travail o' noble lagomorph.* Gravity is about to make a delivery!" Flipping his tail, Sylvester scampered up the tunnel and disappeared.

Moments later, the tunnel shook and a stream of acorns arrived. Horace worked fast, catching the acorns in his paws, laying them on cedar boughs. When one row was full he covered it with boughs and started a new row. At the very moment the storehouse was full, when there wasn't room for one more acorn, they stopped coming.

The tunnel was still. The air smelled sweetly of cedar. Horace went outside, sat on his haunches, and stared at the sky. He thought about Gravity—how strong he must be to keep rocks from flying up and the moon from tumbling down "Does Gravity have a long tail?" he wondered. "What color is his fur? Does he know Mother Nature?"

Clouds scuttled past big trees.

Branches, brittle with ice, rattled in the wind.

Snow fell, stopped, fell again.

The moon, bursting with pride, glowed luminously.

Still Horace stared at the sky.

Still Horace thought about Gravity.

CHAPTER 10

"Yoo-hoo!" Sylvester shouted into the hole. "Wake up, lazybones! Time to drum up some business. Time to make S & H Construction a household name. You haven't poked your whiskers out for three days. I thought it was just bears and sloths that were afflicted by winter sleep disorder. Evidently lagomorphs also suffer the same soporific malaise."

Horace yawned, lifted a paw, and rubbed his eyes. The more he slept, the more he wanted to sleep.

"No wonder you're so lethargic," Sylvester dropped into the tunnel and sniffed the walls. "Imagine living in a damp, dank, dark hovel so far from sun and wind and sky. No thank you. I'll stick to loftier, arboreal domiciles. Come," he held out a paw to Horace. "Come outside my friend, fill your lungs with fresh forest air."

The sky was clear, the wind biting cold. Horace blinked. Glare from the moon hurt his eyes.

"How are the acorns?" Sylvester brushed snow from Horace's coat. "No ordinary nuts are these. Each specimen has been handpicked from special proprietary oaks that have been in my family for generations. Unparalleled flavor and digestibility. Mums the word," he put a paw to his lips. "And that dastardly weasel, if he pokes his snout around here again I'll give him a souvenir he won't soon forget!" he punched the air. "Are you ready for your elocution lesson?"

"Noitucole?" Horace licked the snow.

"Elocution, or verbal articulation as it's sometimes called," Sylvester explained, "is the art of speaking. Pronunciation. Timbre. Voice cadence. Conversation. Repartee. If you're going to represent S & H Construction, you need to impress clients not only with your prodigious digging ability but also your verbal charm. Forgive me for saying this, but your oratorical skills are a corporate liability. If clients hear you speak, they'll do business with our competitors!"

Leaping tree to tree, limb to limb, Sylvester led Horace to a clearing.

"That," Sylvester pointed at a stump, "was once the Sacred Yew, the mightiest tree in the Great Forest. A tree so tall its branches touched the clouds. A tree so eloquent songbirds fought over its crown branch. As you can see by the charred bark, it was hit by lightning. Mother Nature was so upset by fighting between cottontails and hares that in a pique of anger she torched the yew trees with lightning bolts. Yews, sadly, are now extinct. There hasn't been a yew in the Great Forest or the Great Meadow for more than a hundred possum years."

Horace sniffed the blackened stump. It smelled of earth. Not the top layer, the part that touched the sky, but the place you reached when you dug down until even darkness disappeared. Horace had only been to the dark place one time—when the kits told him if he dug far enough he'd find clover as tall as the trees.

"Come," Sylvester leapt onto the charred stump and bowed. "Come, Ecaroh—isn't that what you call yourself? Join me on stage. What? You're afraid of such a measly height? Why this stump is barely taller than that weasel's ugly head. Coil your legs, leap, bound—do whatever it is lagomorphs do to get airborne."

Horace lumbered forward and jumped. Instead of landing on the stump he tumbled into the snow.

"*Magnifique!*" Sylvester clapped his paws together. "You're not only a sculptor but an acrobat. Such grace. Such aplomb. What a theatrical entrance!"

Horace shook snow from his fur and jumped again. This time his aim was better; he landed on top of the stump and skidded to a stop.

"Well done! Well done, o mighty lagomorph!" Sylvester addressed an imaginary audience. "I can see the marquee now. The Great Forest Vaudevillians. Sylvester the Fearless Flying Squirrel and Horace the Lagomorphian Aerialist. We'll dance," he took Horace's forepaws and waltzed him around the stump, "and sing. Tra-la-la! Tra-la-la! We'll entertain frogs and fireflies, buzzards and big-horned sheep. A modest entry fee—an acorn or two—is not unreasonable for admission to a professional theater troupe.

"Where were we?" Sylvester tapped his head with a paw. "Oh yes, elocution and S & H Construction. If you're going to be a partner in this enterprise, you need to be verbally eloquent. Verbal eloquence begins with proper breathing. Not the shallow breathing one does involuntarily, but deep resonant breathing that comes from the diaphragm. From here," he poked Horace's belly. "Take six and a half deep breaths."

Horace yawned.

"Not through the mouth, through the nose! If clients see those incisors we won't have a business!"

Horace closed his mouth and breathed deeply. Loud whistling sounds came from his flared nostrils.

"Admirable, laudable," Sylvester slapped Horace's shoulder. "Not mere lungs have you, but bellows! Not that I would have expected any less. I've taught all the best public speakers in the Great Forest. Except predators, of course. No matter how many acorns a predator offers me, I won't tutor him. It's a matter of principle. Other creatures, those with kind and gentle dispositions, I teach gladly.

Even pro bono, if a creature is indigent. I've mentored countless songbirds. And chipmunks, my distant cousins. I even taught a deer with a speech impediment. He gave a brilliant performance, right here on this stump. One of my pupils, a shy skunk named Justine, went on tour. She gave theatrical performances as far away as the Great Sand Mountain.

"Now then," Sylvester brushed snow from Horace's tail, "you are, I believe, ready to begin formal training. Using the same belly-breathing technique you just demonstrated so admirably, say *bobaboo*. *Bobaboo* tones the vocal cords. *Bobaboo* enhances voice resonance. Once you master *bobaboo,* words will trip over themselves to get out your mouth. Don't worry. I too, was once shy. Instead of talking, I whispered. Instead of emoting, I mumbled. That, of course, was before I mastered the art of elocution. The voice, Horace, is an architectural wonder. From a tiny aperture—the throat—come sounds more powerful than thunder. Sounds that uplift the spirit. Sounds that will, if necessary, assail a malevolent predator. Go ahead. Say it. Say *bobaboo*."

"*Bobaboo*," whispered Horace.

"Louder!" cried Sylvester.

"*Bobaboo*," Horace whispered again.

"For beaver-sake!" Sylvester slapped the stump with his tail. "You're not a spider, you're a lagomorph. A lagomorph with the stature of a black bear. Stop mumbling. Hurl your voice!"

Sylvester flew from the stump to the ground. With a quick, graceful motion, he scooped up and threw a pawful of snow. The icy missile hit Horace's left ear.

"Ouch!" Horace winced from the blow.

"That's better. Now say *bobaboo* the way you said *ouch*."

"*Bobaboo*," said Horace, rubbing his ear.

"What?" Sylvester picked up another pawful of snow. "What did you say?"

"*Bobaboo*!" Horace yelped in pain as a second snowball hit his scabbed-over right ear. "*Bobaboo*!"

"Bravo!" cried Sylvester. "Just as I suspected. You have a magnificent voice. A rich baritone that would make a moose jealous. Now say *oobabob*. I believe that's how you say it. Your penchant for saying words backward has not escaped my attention."

"*Oobabob*," said Horace. It was easier backward than frontward.

"What?" Sylvester made another snowball. "What did you call me?"

"*Oobabob!*" Horace screamed so loud a towhee, watching from a nearby tree, nearly fell from her perch. "*Oobabob!*"

A half-eaten moon dawdled across the Great Forest sky. As moonlight illuminated the clearing, Sylvester had Horace recite different words—mellifluous, delectable, stupendous, beatific, auspicious. Only after each word was shouted so loudly it could be heard at the farthest edge of the clearing did Sylvester let Horace rest.

"Well done, my friend, well done," Sylvester leaped onto the stump and patted Horace's back. "Take a bow. Acknowledge the audience. Can you hear the applause? What an ovation you're getting. Once you've bowed, come off the stage and have a treat. You deserve it after that performance. I know a place so hidden and secluded even I don't know where it is. The greens are as sweet as mother's milk. Tree bark is laced with honey. Water tastes like mead. By the way, did Mother Nature find you? She was looking for you the other day."

Horace knew about Mother Nature. Mother said Mother Nature made cottontail kits. Father said Mother Nature made clouds and the Great Pine. The kits said Mother Nature made blackberries and honey.

"Ah, Mother Nature," Sylvester's eyes glistened reverentially. "What a beauty she is. Gets younger and more radiant every season. They say it's the water she drinks, an elixir made from rainbows and morning dew. As you can imagine, the precise formula for the elixir is much coveted. A crow, trying to cash in on creatures' vain quests for youth and beauty, has been selling a product he calls Mother Nature Water. The crow—Doctor Panacea, he calls himself—claims that if you drink Mother Nature Water every day at sunrise you'll have the gift of eternal life."

Moonlight wriggled though the big trees, casting Horace's shadow upon the snow. The shadow was thin. The meager forage had made him gaunt.

"It's a hoax, a scam, of course," Sylvester scoffed. "Doctor Panacea's elixir is less than worthless. Only Mother Nature lives forever. The rest of us are flawed, bickering over acorns and blades of grass."

CHAPTER 11

Each night, shortly after darkness shrouded the Great Forest, Sylvester led Horace to the clearing. There, atop the stump of the Sacred Yew, he gave him elocution lessons. He taught Horace phrases to use when talking to prospective clients: "All work comes with an acorn-back guarantee. S & H Construction— affordable and dependable subterranean domiciles. We reserve the right to refuse service to ferrets and weasels."

He made Horace memorize proverbs and lines of poetry: "So you will sound intelligent, unlike our slovenly and boorish competitors. Your elegant snow sculptures clearly demonstrate your artistic gifts. Poetry and song are but further embellishments to your refined disposition."

Horace turned his ears and listened to the wind.

"Exquisite. Melodic. A virtuosic performance," Sylvester said after a moonless night when Horace recited a poem about a ladybug and a spider. "Your diction was superb, the audience enthralled. A family of wrens was in attendance, also a groundhog and three possums. A field mouse was so moved she broke down in tears."

Horace tumbled off the stump and drank from a puddle of water. Melting snow revealed more and more of the Great Forest. Shrubs, bushes, and thickets were shedding their winter coats. Paths and runs, hidden since the first winter storm, appeared as if by magic. Osoberry, a hardy and precocious harbinger of spring, had tiny green buds.

"Mother Nature," Sylvester counted the rings of the stump with his tail, "has decided to bring spring early this year. I'm told it has something to do with a malfunction in her weather pouch. Unfortunately, the dampness," he groaned and lifted a stiff paw, "is aggravating my ague. I'll be leaving soon for drier, more hospitable climes. I have a little *pied-à-terre* on the Great Sand Mountain. Nothing fancy, just a bole in an ash tree and a cache of pine nuts. A place to dry out and give my aching bones a rest."

"*Pied-à-terre?*" Horace stumbled over the strange words. "*Erret-a-deip?*"

"*Pied,*" Sylvester raised a paw, "is the French word for foot. *Terre,*" he slapped the ground with his tail, "is the French word for earth. Hence *pied-à-terre,* a place to put down one's feet. I come from a long line of polyglots—creatures who speak many languages. I know seventeen different tongues and dialects. Eighteen, if you include the language of two-leggeds."

"Legs," Horace giggled and pointed at his feet, "talk."

"What! You mean to say you don't know what a two-legged is? A two-legged—may you never have the misfortune to encounter one—is a vicious predator. More dangerous than a ferret, a skunk, or even that weasel you dispatched. Two-leggeds walk like this"— Sylvester stood on his hind legs, "and smell like this"—he pinched his nose. "Instead of growing their own fur, they kill creatures and wear their pelts!"

A dark shadow passed over the clearing. Sylvester leaped from the stump to the ground. Tail billowing, he sprinted across the clearing, climbed a madrone tree, and disappeared.

Horace shivered. His nose and ears and eyes scanned the darkness. The shadow made three slow, hypnotic circles. Suddenly, like a shooting star, it plummeted from the sky. Feathers flattened against its bones, hooked beak slicing through darkness, the shadow streaked toward Horace.

"*Bobaboo!*" The word Sylvester made Horace shout from the stump of the Sacred Yew leaped from his throat. "*Oobabob!*"

Bobaboo! and *oobabob!* hit the streaking owl like bolts of lightning. It jackknifed and doubled back. Careening wildly between the trees, it crossed the Lesser Stream and disappeared into the Great Meadow.

A feather, teased by gusts of wind, floated from sky to earth. Horace pinned it beneath a giant paw. The feather was gray and black. Iridescent green specks radiated from the shaft.

Horace sniffed the feather and pawed it repeatedly. Satisfied it was dead, he carried it to his tunnel and mounted it triumphantly between Snow-Mother and Snow-Father.

CHAPTER 12

The blizzard was a mistake. Mother Nature reached into her weather pouch and pulled out what she thought were spring showers. Instead of gentle showers, cold air, gale force winds, sleet, and snow assaulted the Great Forest. Limbs snapped. Branches sheared off. Uprooted and unearthed, trees crashed to the forest floor.

Horace was foraging when the blizzard struck. He tried to shelter under the cedar but Mother Nature drove him back. She made icicles of his whiskers and flattened his ears with her howling winds. Frightened by the ferocity of the storm, he crawled into his tunnel and put trembling paws over his eyes.

Three nights and four days Horace stayed in the tunnel. He slept, ate acorns and roots from the storehouse, then slept again. On the fourth day, he had a dream. In the dream he was being chased by cloud-creatures. Not playful cloud-creatures like those Mother showed him, but cloud-creatures with snares, bows, knives, and axes—weapons Sylvester said two-leggeds used to kill creatures and tear off their fur. The cloud-creatures chased Horace until he was so exhausted he fell from the sky. He fell through dark, angry clouds, snow and hail, lightning and thunder. Below him, he saw Mother and Father. They tried to catch him, but he slipped through their outstretched paws.

⌒

"GOODNESS GOPHERS!" MOTHER NATURE TURNED TO HER assistants, the Merry Little Breezes. "It's that runt cottontail, the one I gifted shyness and silence. Why is he sobbing like that? How did he get so big? And how on earth did he end up in the Great Forest? I thought I made it clear cottontails and hares were to stay away from each other. That's why I made the Lesser Stream—to separate the clans and keep them from feuding. Such sadness on his whiskers. He looks cold and hungry too. I can't just leave him like that."

Mother Nature put cold air, howling winds, sleet, and snow flurries back in her weather pouch. In their place, she took out stillness and warm air. "It's the least I can do after mistakenly pulling out that storm," she told the Merry Little Breezes. "I do hope creatures will forgive me."

Calm slowly settled over the Great Forest. Driven into holes and caves by the blizzard, residents cautiously left the safety of their refuges. Birds pecked ice from their nests. Moles broke through thawing earth. Rivulets of water, frozen on their way to the Lesser Stream, began running and singing again. Snow-milk thistle and snow-clover sagged and drooped. Snow-Mother and Snow-Father became piles of slush. The owl feather toppled into the muddied snow.

Mother Nature was in a hurry. She was needed other places. Places where plants and creatures were closer to spring. Places where the earth needed thawing and buds were yearning to swell. There was the Great Sand Mountain with its crags, aeries, and cliffs. And the Ancient Bog. And the open lea of the Great Meadow. All anxiously awaited Mother Nature's arrival.

"What's his name again?" Mother Nature frowned at the Merry Little Breezes for playing tag with gusts of wind, "the one that looks so sad, the puma-sized cottontail? Morris? Or perhaps Boris? No, that's not it. Now I remember, it's Horace. I never will understand why cottontails choose such old-fashioned names."

Mother Nature did one more thing before hurrying from the Great Forest—she sprinkled magic dust on Horace's coat.

"I gave him a double-dusting," she told the Merry Little Breezes. "He'll need it to cross the Lesser Stream and find his way home."

CHAPTER 13

nstinct was Horace's guide. Instinct and the magic dust Mother Nature sprinkled on his coat. Instead of trudging through the densest part of the Great Forest, he circled big trees, followed trails and runs revealed by the recently melted snow. He avoided root balls unearthed by the storm, crawled under dense brush, found seams and openings through snowdrifts hidden from sun. When he came to a fork in the trail he stopped, looked at the sky, and asked Celestial Cottontails which way to go. Winking and shooting across the sky, the ancestors guided him.

It was raining when Horace reached the Lesser Stream. Where the bank met the rushing water he stopped, lowered his head, and drank. Icy, snow-fed water splashed across his face and ran down his throat. He drank ravenously, lapping at the water as though it were succulent meadow grass. Close to shore was a bar of gravel and sand. Farther out, in the middle of the stream, rocks jutted from the rapids. Beyond the rapids lay blue, treeless sky and open meadow.

The first steps were easy. Horace touched one rock and moved quickly to the next. But as he got farther from shore, the rocks changed. They didn't jut as far above the water and were slick with moss. Instead of gripping the rocks, the pads of his feet slid across them. Near midstream, he fell into the rapids.

The Lesser Stream tossed Horace around like he was a twig. It threw him into the air, flipped him tail over paws, and tumbled him downstream. Churning brown water crashed over his head. Banks swept past in a blur of spray and foam.

Horace passed through the rapids, into the main channel of the stream. Here, where the current wasn't as swift, he was able to keep his head above water. Clawing with his forepaws, kicking with his hind paws, he moved slowly toward the far bank. But each time the shoreline drew close, he was swept downstream again. Battling the angry water sapped Horace's strength. His head drooped. His legs grew heavy. It became harder and harder to breathe. Relentlessly, the Lesser Stream imposed its will.

A willow tree, bowed by the current, saved Horace. A branch, rising above the rapids, snagged him as he went past. Digging his claws into the bark, he inched his way across the branch and dropped ashore.

Horace lay unmoving on the bank. His ears twitched. His eyes wandered. The roar of angry water thundered in his head. When his panting slowed, he crawled uphill until he came to a thicket. Flattening himself out, he crawled under brambles and dried himself with a weary tongue.

Through an opening in the thicket, Horace watched the Lesser Stream rush past. He watched warily, the way a creature watches a fleeing predator after narrowly escaping its grasp.

CHAPTER 14

The Lesser Stream was in a foul mood. Bloated and raging, it had swept Horace downstream, dashed him against rocks, and tried to drown him. Now, watching from the safety of the thicket, Horace discovered water had different moods. When the rain slowed, the stream didn't rush so fast or claw so viciously at the banks. When the sky cleared, its voice was softer, gentler. Sometimes, it even called his name. "Horace Cottontail," the Lesser Stream called, "Ecaroh Liatnottoc. Don't sit there on the bank. Come down and play."

Night and day, the Lesser Stream prattled. It told stories. It bragged and gossiped. Mostly, it plundered. Horace watched the foaming brown water attack the banks and carry off everything that wasn't deeply rooted. He witnessed its upstream looting too: stumps, logs, branches, bushes—even the bloated carcass of a dead elk—rushed past.

The Lesser Stream was a watering hole and gathering place. Deer, porcupine, skunk, possum, and creatures Horace didn't recognize came to drink and bathe. Some came from the Great Forest, some from the Great Meadow. A few, like a family of river otters, went back and forth between the two banks. Horace felt safe inside the thicket. It was dense and close to the ground. Sharp thorns kept out all but the smallest creatures. Beetles and ants lived under a mound of dirt. A bee slept beneath a pile of leaves.

On a night the Lesser Stream was in a good mood, Horace left the thicket and went down to the water. Careful to stay close to the bank, he bathed and drank. Bending over to drink, he saw a creature. First he thought it was a fish. Then he thought it was an otter. When the moon rose he realized the creature looking back at him was a cottontail. He put a paw in the water and tried to touch it, but it darted away. The same thing happened over and over again; no matter how fast he pawed at the cottontail, it was always gone.

The moon fattened slowly, like a ripening blackberry. The moon in the Great Forest, hidden by big trees, was small and shy. Sometimes it barely reached the cedar tree or the entrance to Horace's tunnel. This moon, reflected in the boisterous water, was huge and bright. "Is this the moon that lives in the Great Meadow?" Horace wondered. "Is this the moon that sleeps above the Great Pine? Are Mother and Father looking at the same moon I am?" Thinking about Mother and Father made Horace shiver with excitement. Thinking about Mother and Father made him want to try and cross the Lesser Stream again.

Horace left the thicket and went to the top of the bank. Moonlight gave the water a silver sheen. Water lapped at the far bank, washed across rocks jutting from the stream. "The moon isn't afraid of water," Horace thought. "The moon crosses whenever it wants. The moon even plays in the rapids."

Horace took six deep belly breaths—like Sylvester made him do before every elocution lesson. Determined to leap across the churning water and reach the open meadow, he hurtled down the bank. Halfway down he tripped, somersaulted, and landed in the icy stream. Shaking water from his fur, he climbed the bank, and ran down the hill again. This time he landed close to a jutting rock.

The rock gave him an idea. *I'll build a bridge across the water,* he thought. *I'll walk across the bridge to the other side.*

Excited by his plan, Horace rolled rocks down the bank and piled them up in the water. The first pile, close to shore, was two rocks high. The second pile, farther into the stream, was three rocks high. It was hard work. The rocks were heavy, and the farther he got from shore, the taller each pile had to be to rise above the water. He worked through the night, and by daybreak had reached midstream. Confident he'd soon be able to cross, he went back to the thicket and slept.

Wakening before the sun, Horace hurried down the bank.

The rocks he'd so laboriously piled up were gone.

Churning brown water had washed away his bridge.

CHAPTER 15

The ground beneath the thicket opened and a tiny head appeared. "Pardon me," said a wee voice, "but I believe you may be sitting on one of my tunnels."

The creature was smaller than one of Horace's paws. It had gray ears, shiny black eyes, and a tail twice as long as its body. Its coat was grayish brown and shaggy. Its belly and legs were pink.

"*Mea culpa*," Horace rose from the thicket. "Excuse me. Beg your pardon. Sorry. *Je suis désolée.*"

Sylvester taught Horace to apologize—it was part of the elocution lessons. "Customers," Sylvester said, "are right even when they're wrong. Apologies are good for business."

"Please, please," begged the tiny creature, "do stay where you are. I didn't mean to displace you. I simply wanted to call the tunnel to your attention in case the ground suddenly gave way. It's not a tunnel I use very often. Only in emergencies or when there's a cave-in someplace."

"Excavation, demolition, renovation," Horace said. "Reasonable rates. Prompt service. All work comes with an acorn-back guarantee."

"It's very kind of you to offer," the creature looked admiringly at Horace's paws, "but it won't be necessary. Making and mending tunnels is one of my regular chores. Tunnels collapse all the time, especially when the water is high. Besides, my tunnels are barely wide enough for a vole to squeeze through. A female vole, that is," she added with a giggle. "By the way," she licked her tiny paws with a tiny pink tongue, "there are nettles at the top of the bank. They're still below ground so you might not have noticed them. Come spring they'll be towering over your head."

"Seltten," Horace said. He remembered how Mother chewed nettles then put them in his mouth. He remembered too, how nettles made his tongue tingle.

"I hope this doesn't sound rude," the vole said, "but how did you get so big? I've never seen a cottontail with your stature. And how did you get on this side of the Lesser Stream? As far as I know, cottontails live exclusively in the Great Meadow."

"Owl," trembling at the memory, Horace pointed at the sky. "Lwo."

"Oh dear!" cried the vole. "Oh goodness, dear! What a dreadful thing to happen. Thank gophers you're all right. I sometimes have nightmares where I'm abducted by a kingfisher." Her body shook and the gray-brown fur on her back stood straight out from her pink skin.

When the vole stopped shaking she said, "Let's talk about more pleasant things, shall we? Like the Lesser Stream. It's changing, you know. Last night, for the first time in two moons, I crossed without risking my life. Not being able to go back and forth has been a great imposition. Especially when there's horsetail fern on the other side. I adore horsetail fern."

Horace stared curiously at the tiny creature. She didn't have wings. She didn't have fins. "How can she cross the angry rushing water?" he wondered.

"I'm a water vole," she anticipated his thoughts. "I'm often confused with my cousins, the shrews, who live exclusively on land. Or my other cousins, the field mice. Or my rat cousins who have, unfortunately, a very bad reputation. You may have noticed my long tail. It makes a useful rudder. My flared snout allows me to breathe under water. Not that I spend much time down there—just long enough to make the crossing. I prefer living on the banks. The vegetation suits me, and I can swim when I feel the urge. Though it's not something I do regularly, and certainly not for pleasure or amusement. If there's better forage on the forest bank, I'll be here. If there's better forage on the meadow bank, I'll be on the other side. I maintain domiciles on both banks. Everything, of course, depends on the weather. That and Mother Nature."

"Mother Nature makes cottontails," Horace remembered Mother's voice, how her whiskers trembled when she told Mother Nature stories. "Mother Nature makes cloud-creatures and butterflies."

"Mother Nature is very clever," the vole made a murmuring sound, "and very wise. As you've probably heard, she's been delayed. Spring won't come until she gets here and warms things up."

The vole moved a few tail lengths away and chewed a blackberry cane. She worked in a very orderly manner, stripping bark from one side of the cane before moving around and stripping the other side. After chewing the cane, she moved pulp from her mouth to her paws. Only when both paws were full did she move pulp back to her mouth and eat.

"Goodness gophers!" The vole lifted a paw and daintily brushed crumbs from her lips. "I do hope you'll excuse my rudeness. I've been so busy talking and eating I haven't even introduced myself. Meandra Cassandra Volare Vole is my name. My friends call me Meandra."

"Horace Cottontail," Horace patted the top of his head. "Ecaroh Liatnottoc. A pleasure and honor. Horace rhymes with Boris," he was careful to enunciate the way Sylvester taught him. "Boris rhymes with Horace."

"Horace. What a lovely name!" Meandra clapped her tiny paws together. "The most beautiful I've ever heard!"

"The pleasure, Madame," Horace remembered exactly how the phrase sounded when recited from the stump of the Sacred Yew, "is all mine."

"I do believe," the vole blinked as she spoke, "that we shall be friends. Fast friends. I can always tell. Mother Nature gave me exceptional instincts. I know when fair weather is coming and when a storm is approaching. I know when tender shoots are about to burst from the earth. I also know when a friend, a true friend, comes into my life."

Horace blushed. His lips, cheeks, nose—and even the tips of his ears—turned red. If Meandra Cassandra Volare Vole were bigger, if she came up to his foot or even just the pad of his paw, he would have nuzzled her.

CHAPTER 16

M eandra was right—the Lesser Stream was changing. It still hurried past and gnawed on the banks, but its voice was weaker and its foul moods didn't last as long. Boulders in the middle of the stream were partially exposed. Except for the base of its trunk, the willow that saved Horace was out of the water. When Horace drank or bathed, the water-cottontail looking back at him didn't run away as fast.

Now that the Lesser Stream was calmer, Meandra spent more time on the meadow bank. The rich forage suited her. She was bigger. Her coat was shinier. She ate in a more relaxed manner. The forest bank, Horace's new home, changed. A green frog moved into a hole in the trunk of an alder tree. Newts with orange bellies crawled out of the water and lazed on rocks. The bee left the thicket. A family of snakes moved under a rotting log.

Horace thought a great deal about the time he spent in the Great Forest. Even though he'd been cold and hungry much of the time, it was an exciting adventure. He met Sylvester and had elocution lessons. He dug a tunnel and made a storehouse for the acorns. He even overcame his fear of the owl. Once he discovered he could drive it away by yelling "Bobaboo!" he sometimes wished it would come back—just so he could drive it away again. The feather that floated from the sky, the one he put between Snow-Mother and Snow-Father, wilted and sagged. The once showy plumage, Horace noted with satisfaction, would never fly again, never terrorize another creature.

Two fat moons after being battered and regurgitated by the Lesser Stream, Horace was foraging nettle shoots along the top of the bank. In the distance, he heard yipping and yapping. As the yips and yaps grew louder, he became increasingly wary. His nostrils flared. His ears twitched. His fur bristled.

A coyote, ears pinned against its head, bounded out of the Great Forest.

His entire life, Horace had been clumsy. Instead of moving gracefully, he tumbled and plodded. Instead of leaping and bounding, he tripped and somersaulted. Now, propelled by fear, he ran so fast his paws barely touched the ground. He ran upstream until the coyote cut him off. He ran downstream but the coyote cut him off again. He ran in circles, zigged and zagged, sprang into the air, changed directions. Whatever he did, wherever he went, the coyote blocked his way.

The coyote herded Horace into a narrow opening. On one side was a wall of driftwood, on the other side a rock outcropping. Above him, saliva dripping from its jowls, stood the snarling beast. Behind him, dark and foreboding, was the Lesser Stream. Horace looked anxiously back and forth between the snarling beast and the churning water. Then he bounded into the water.

The Lesser Stream pulled Horace under, swept him downstream. But this time the current was weaker and the rapids more subdued. Horace thrashed and kicked until he rose to the surface. Then he paddled. Instead of trying to go straight across the water, he swam at an angle. Instead of fighting the current, he let it carry him. Clawing with his forelegs and kicking with his hind legs, he moved slowly toward the far bank, the yips and yaps growing ever distant.

When, shivering and exhausted, Horace reached shore he was greeted by a familiar voice.

"Bravo. Bravo, my brave friend," Meandra Cassandra Volare Vole poked her tiny head out of a hole in the mud. "Welcome to the land of horsetail fern. Welcome to the Great Meadow."

CHAPTER 17

Meadow ground felt familiar under paw. The red clay was the same that lined the warren tunnels. Teasel and mugwort were kin to plants that grew near the blackberry thicket. The heavy-scented greenery of the Great Meadow, an aroma Horace could only yearn for and imagine during the long winter in the Great Forest, rose fresh and pungent in his nostrils.

Horace foraged as he traveled. He ate plantain, dandelion, chickweed, and owl's clover. Though small, the greens were sweet and tender. He nibbled miner's lettuce, chewed purple berries from scrub juniper, licked dew flavored with pennyroyal. The rich meadow forage sated him. After months of constant hunger his stomach was relaxed and content.

Horace felt the Great Pine before he saw it. He felt the Great Pine the way songbirds feel it when they're tired and need to rest, the way wind feels it after a long journey from the Great Sand Mountain. He felt its crown branch turning in the breeze. He felt its smell, the sound of its rustling needles, the cast of its ponderous shadow falling nearly to the Ancient Bog.

Even more than its towering presence, it was the Great Pine's aura, the way it was revered, that made it memorable. Parents took newborns—kits, fawns, cubs, calves, pups—on pilgrimages to the Great Pine. Beset by famine or illness, creatures large and small sought the tree's blessing. They asked for protection from enemies, medicinal plants to alleviate pain, food to stave off hunger.

Over generations of moons, the Great Pine's trunk had become wrinkled and fissured. Deer and elk had rubbed their antlers against it. Wind and rain had lashed it. Lightning had blackened it. Creatures had gnawed it. Beads of pitch glistened from the wounds.

Horace went to the root hollow. The root hollow was the secret cottontail hiding place. Kits slept in the root hollow while their mothers spun thistledown and gathered pine nuts. Father made kits dive into the root hollow as part of their survival training.

The root hollow was filled with winter debris—leaves, grass, dirt, twigs, bark. Horace kicked everything out and crawled inside. Then he reached up, pulled pine needles over the opening, and slept. Not a restless, troubled sleep like those he'd endured under the snowbank, but a deep, peaceful sleep from which he awoke rested and invigorated.

During the winter in the Great Forest, Horace shivered from cold and dampness. Now, he shivered with excitement. He was nearly home. Soon he'd see Mother and Father, sleep in his this-tledown bed, play with the kits. He'd tell them how the owl carried him across the sky. He'd tell them how he met Sylvester, learned elocution on the stump of the Sacred Yew, outran a coyote, and crossed the angry water of the Lesser Stream.

Nose quivering, ears turning, Horace searched the sky for danger. Guided by instinct and memory, he left the Great Pine and moved toward the blackberry thicket and the warren.

CHAPTER 18

Horace knew when a path was about to turn or twist, where it would join another path, go uphill or downhill. He knew a stand of wild roses was ahead before the scent of wild roses reached his nostrils. He knew the hollow ash tree where bees stored honey was approaching before he smelled the honey. He knew because this was his place in the world. Horace was part of the Great Meadow. The Great Meadow was part of Horace.

Warm rain, falling from Mother Nature's weather pouch, danced on Horace's coat. Elated, he stuck out his tongue and drank from the sky. He felt giddy, light-headed. He grunted. He hummed. He shook his ears from side to side. Instead of walking or hopping, he skipped. When he saw a slug on the trail he greeted it with a bow. "Good evening, esteemed Mr. Slug," he recited the words exactly as Sylvester had taught them during elocution lessons. "May your journey, however slow, be fruitful and exhilarating."

When Horace was abducted by the owl, the Great Meadow was blanketed with snow. Every tree and path, every breath and paw print was part of the glistening whiteness. Now the earth was green. Not one shade of green but hundreds of different hues. Green was not a color; it was a proclamation. "Mother Nature has arrived!" the earth shouted. "Spring has come to the Great Meadow!"

Horace came to the downed log, the place of his greatest joy and greatest sorrow. Here, in this very spot, the kits had catapulted off his shoulders and called him "Dumb Bunny the Great!" During the loneliness of winter in the Great Forest the memory of those four words had given him hope. One night, homesick and sad, he'd shouted "Dumb Bunny the Great!" to the vacant sky. An echo, a distant reply from the depths of the shrouded forest, had raised his sunken spirits. Here too, beneath this downed log, he'd been separated from everything he loved. In one brief instant, as the owl's talons knifed into his flanks, he'd been snatched from the comfort of earth and delivered to the terror of sky.

The log was bare, snow replaced by moss and bark. Horace circled the log, sniffing and remembering. He stood below the log, closed his eyes, and imagined the feel of paws on his shoulders. Those paws, paws of brothers, sisters, and playmates, would soon welcome him home.

The brush behind the log rustled. Zephyros, a frail withered, cottontail elder appeared. His chin whiskers were gray, the fur on his back thin and patchy.

"I'm afraid I must give you sad news," Zephyros put a tremulous paw on Horace's shoulder. "Shortly after you disappeared, your father was killed by a lynx. He was searching for you on the Great Sand Mountain. You've come at a dangerous time. It's mating season. The bucks, crazed with jealousy, are fighting over does. Whatever you do, stay away from the warren."

Horace went back to the root hollow in a daze. Even during the loneliest days in the Great Forest, he never felt so sad.

GREEN NEEDLES SHOT OUT FROM THE BRANCHES OF THE Great Pine. Spring pitch, fresh and clear, oozed from the trunk. Bats clouded the night sky. Ants mounded up dirt until their nest was taller than Horace's head.

Horace barely noticed the changes. He was too busy thinking about Father. The way Father leaped to snag huckleberries from a bush. The way Father walked without bending a blade of grass and sat as still as a stone while the moon crossed the sky. He thought about Father's smell and voice and the feel of his nose.

On a windy, humid night with dark clouds hiding moon and stars, a summer storm fell from Mother Nature's weather pouch. Thunder bellowed. Lightning flashed above the Great Sand Mountain. The Great Pine groaned and swayed. Though terrified, Horace didn't hide or cover his eyes. He wanted to show Father he was brave.

The storm ended. The air was still. The Great Pine stood calm and silent. Celestial Cottontails—cottontails who died and became stars—blanketed the sky. There were so many stars Horace couldn't tell which one was Father. Was he bright or dim, near or far, big or small?

A solitary star suddenly streaked across the sky. Blazing and sparkling, it left the other stars in a dim wake. As the blazing star disappeared, tears streamed down Horace's cheeks.

Consumed with grief, Horace returned to the root hollow beneath the Great Pine.

Nestled in pine needles was a braid of Mother's fur.

CHAPTER 19

Horace missed cottontail voices. He missed the click of Mother's tongue, the whir of air whistling through Father's teeth, the shrill laughter of the kits. During the loneliness of winter in the Great Forest, he sometimes heard familiar voices. Thinking Mother and Father had come to take him home, he followed the sounds into the big trees. All he found were moaning limbs and lowing wind.

The voices Horace heard now were coming from the Ancient Bog, a low-lying fen between the Great Pine and the Lower Swale. Following the sounds, he came to a grove of cottonwood trees. Beyond the cottonwoods, on a mound of peat, was a circle of cottontail bucks. In the middle of the circle two bucks were boxing. Standing on their hind legs, the boxers jabbed, punched, feinted, and dodged. Sometimes they flew into the air and kicked with their hind legs. When a boxer landed a blow, bucks in the circle cheered and thumped their tails on the peat. Moonlight bathed the spectacle in a soft golden light.

Mesmerized by the voices and boxing, Horace forgot to be wary. Cottontails were suddenly behind him, nipping at his heels.

Yipping and clicking their tongues, they drove him onto the bog, into the circle of cheering bucks.

One of the boxers was Juniper, a kit who bounced off Horace's shoulders when they played Leap Bunny in the snow. No longer a kit, Juniper was now a full-grown buck with sturdy legs and a muscular chest. The other boxer was a tall, quick-footed buck with a black crest on his chest.

"Look who's here!" Juniper hissed. "It's Dumb Bunny. With his head full of stupidity! Have you come to fight? Have you come to woo the does with your clumsiness?"

Horace bared his neck, a sign of respect and affection in the cottontail clan. Instead of baring his neck, Juniper bared his teeth.

"Dumb Bunny!" the bucks in the circle chanted. "Dumb Bunny! Dumb Bunny!"

"Come on, coward!" Juniper shoved Horace. "Show us what a great boxer you are. Show us you deserve the most beautiful does."

Chanting voices rose above the miasma of the bog.

"Clobber the idiot!"

"Smash his fat head!"

"Flatten the oaf!"

The black-crested buck butted Horace and raised a menacing paw.

"Back up!" Juniper threw the black-crested buck aside. "I'll handle this numbskull!"

Goaded by the chanting, Juniper punched Horace's chest and pummeled his flanks. A blow from his foot hit Horace's leg.

Horace moaned and dropped to the turf. Burning pain shot up his leg. Tears clouded his eyes.

"Dumb Bunny! Dumb Bunny!" the bucks chanted.

"Coward!" Juniper punched Horace's limp body. "Get up and fight!"

Horace covered his eyes with his paws.

As Juniper charged, his head slammed into Horace's out-stretched paws. Twisting in the air, he crumpled to the peat.

The chanting ceased. Bucks in the circle stared numbly at their fallen leader.

"Hawks! Hawks!" Warning cries, loud and piercing beneath the midsummer moon, came from the branches of the cottonwood trees. "Run for your lives!"

Terrified cottontail eyes nervously searched the sky.

Cottonwood trees sighed. Teasel stalks rustled. The smell of drying peat drifted across the bog.

Like a fleeing wind, the bucks disappeared into the summer night.

CHAPTER 20

Sylvester raced down the cottonwood, catapulted off a limb, and landed gracefully on the peat.

"Rise, Horace, rise! Lift your mighty paws, o noble lagomorph! Don't worry—there isn't a hawk between here and the Mighty River. My father, may he repose in plentitude, taught me to imitate forty-seven different winged creatures. What a battle you fought—slaying that brute like he was a gnat. Not that I would have expected any less. I remember well the day you drove off that thieving weasel. Nothing you do surprises me. Nothing!"

Horace lay trembling on the peat. His eyes were closed. Blood trickled down his injured leg. Next to him, unmoving, lay Juniper.

"Thank gophers you're all right," Sylvester brushed Horace's injured leg with his tail. "Nothing broken, I hope. The head intact? Chin? Nose? Ears? What about the spleen? Don't worry, I know just the thing to stop the bleeding. Let's get off this muck first. It's unpredictable. And downright dangerous!"

Supporting Horace's injured leg with his tail, Sylvester led him off the bog. "Don't move a whisker," he ordered when they reached the cottonwood grove. "I'll be back before you can say acorn stew!"

Sylvester returned with a clump of spider silk in his mouth. "Stuff's amazing," he packed the webbing on Horace's bloodied leg. "A possum I knew got sliced up by a fox. His entire flank was peeled open. Enough blood to make a small pond. I contracted with every spider in the Great Forest, bought their entire inventory of abandoned webs—at a most exorbitant price, I might add—and put the whole sticky mess on the possum's wound. The bleeding stopped faster than you can say *astounding*."

"A mere trifle," Sylvester dismissed Horace's moans with a wave of his paw. "With rest and a few decent meals you'll soon be hopping around like a grasshopper again. Why, you're shaking like a frog's tongue. Here, come around behind this boulder. There's a dastardly draft coming from the southwest. Do you like cleavers? I don't care for them myself but I'm told lagomorphs favor them. What? You're not hungry? As emaciated as you look, you must be starving. Your cheekbones are sharp as a buzzard's beak!"

Sylvester disappeared again. This time he came back with a clump of greens dangling from his mouth. "Eat! Eat!" He dropped the greens in front of Horace. "You need sustenance after dispatching that deranged mob. To say nothing of the brute who attacked you. It's a disgrace the way these bucks carry on, maiming each other to win the affection of a few does. They're a blight on the entire lagomorph clan!"

The cleavers were prickly on the outside and gooey on the inside. Horace didn't like the taste but ate them anyway—to please Sylvester.

"I hadn't planned to be here," Sylvester removed a cleaver sprig clinging to Horace's chin. "I was headed home after a lengthy sabbatical at my *pied-à-terre* on the Great Sand Mountain when a series of unexpected and fortuitous events interrupted my plans. I stopped for a drink at the Mighty River. There I encountered a member of the hare clan. Madrone, I believe he calls himself. He told me you'd been driven from the Great Forest and taken refuge in the Great Meadow. In the interest of maintaining our friendship, I won't repeat the scurrilous things he said about cottontails, how you violated Mother Nature's edict by crossing the Lesser Stream and venturing into hare territory. After fording the Mighty River on a log, I encountered the daughter of a raven I once saved from starvation. She told me she'd just seen you and that you were in dire and dangerous circumstances. Ravens, unlike blackbirds and woodpeckers, are not given to exaggeration."

Horace licked the wound. A thin scab was already beginning to form.

"My great ancestral grandmother," Sylvester adjusted the spider's silk on Horace's injured leg, "had a name for these seemingly random encounters. *Destina*, she called them. *Destina* leads a creature along one path instead of another when it comes to a fork in the trail. *Destina* brings two creatures to the same place at the same time even though neither of them planned to be there. *Destina* makes the wind blow one direction, then suddenly blow the opposite direction. *Destina* is everything unknown and mysterious...."

Sylvester gave a long speech. He talked about the vagaries of weather on the Great Sand Mountain, the wisdom of Mother Nature, the deceitfulness of ferrets and weasels, how elocution builds self-confidence and molds character.

"A stuttering toad came to see me a few moons back," Sylvester put the last of the spider silk on Horace's cut ear. "He had an inferiority complex. Poor fellow couldn't get a glance, much less a wife. After a few elocution sessions he croaked louder than a bull elk and tap-danced on the stump of the Sacred Yew. Once he got over his fear of speaking, he became quite the dandy. He has, I'm told, a harem of female frogs that dote on him night and day. They even catch insects for him—so he doesn't have to move. What were we talking about? Oh yes, *Destina*, how I came to be in the

Great Meadow tonight, how you and I, as different as hazelnuts and hummingbirds, keep bumping into each other. By the way, where did you learn to box like that? That left jab you threw was a thing of beauty. The brute didn't have time to blink!"

Horace didn't hear the rest of Sylvester's speech.

Comforted by the squirrel's familiar voice, he slept.

CHAPTER 21

Sylvester climbed the Great Pine like it was a sapling, spiraling up the massive trunk, swinging limb to limb by his tail. When he reached the crown branch he closed his eyes and swayed. Once the wind calmed, he looked out across the Great Meadow. He saw the Lesser Stream, the Lower Swale, the edges of the Ancient Bog, the Great Sand Mountain. Everything was bathed in moonlight.

"Over there! Closer to the shadow!" Sylvester pitched a pine cone at Horace. "And for newt-sake be quick about it. These widow-maker limbs make me nervous as a dragonfly."

Favoring his injured leg, Horace placed pine cones, paced off the length of the Great Pine's shadow, and dragged a branch around the trunk so it made a circle in the dirt. Sylvester jabbered the whole time, shouting out numbers, converting cottontail paws to squirrel tails, making estimations and approximations.

"The Great Pine isn't going to fall anytime soon," Sylvester spit out a wad of pine needles. "My calculations prove that definitively. Next time that stoat who runs the gambling operation gives me betting odds on the Great Pine's demise, I'll recoup my losses—with acorns of profit! Another thing—those gnaw marks on the trunk weren't made by beavers. Beavers have long, crooked teeth. Their gnaws are messy and irregular. These gouges, you will observe, are small and precise. This is clearly the work of two-leggeds."

"Owt-sdeggel walk like this," Horace tried to stand on his hind legs—the way Sylvester did when he told him about two-leggeds—but fell over and turned a somersault.

"Marvelous, Ecaroh. Marvelous! "Sylvester clapped his paws together. "You've always been laconic—a lagomorph of few if any words. But when you do talk, which is rare, huckleberries of wisdom tumble from your mouth. Don't worry," he waved a dismissive paw. "Your pelt is safe. Those gnaw marks are older than a toothless skunk. Two-leggeds haven't been here for half a possum's age. My maternal great-grandfather, may he repose in plentitude, lived above a two-legged den. From moons of careful observation he gleaned much valuable information about their behavior. Two-leggeds gnaw a tree when they're in love. It's a mating ritual."

Horace was distracted by a ladybug. Feathering her lacy wings, she hovered over the Great Pine's fissured trunk. Instead of crossing the glistening pitch, she made a long detour around it.

"A storm's on the way," Sylvester sniffed the wind suspiciously. "I can feel it in my spleen. Meteorology and astronomy are other subjects for which the squirrel clan is renowned. Did I ever tell you about the time I drove off a hoard of dangerous and malicious foxes? Not with force, but with guile—by correctly calibrating the arrival of an impending lunar eclipse. When the sky suddenly turned black, the foxes turned tail and fled."

The ladybug crawled in and out of creases in the Great Pine's bark. When she disappeared, Horace felt sad. When she reappeared, he clapped his paws with delight.

"I have an idea," Sylvester tugged on his whiskers. "Come back to the Great Forest with me. A cousin of mine checked on your subterranean domicile while I was on sabbatical. He sent me messages with a vacationing dove. Your hole, though filled with debris, is still very much habitable. A bit shabby, to be sure, but nothing a little sweat and ingenuity won't fix. You can rest and heal your wounds. I have all the acorns you can ever eat. It will be like old times."

Lightning flashed across the Great Sand Mountain. The Great Pine was briefly illuminated. Then it was dark again.

Three times Sylvester started to talk. But each time he fell silent.

"Forgive my bluntness," he said at last, "but I must discuss a delicate yet vitally important topic before the onset of inclement weather. Admittedly, this would be better explained by someone in your own clan, but as there is no one here to do it, and you have clearly not been instructed in this matter, I will try. There comes a time when a creature takes a mate. In the squirrel clan this happens in early spring, right after Mother Nature brings the first thaw. Lagomorphs, on the other paw, are evidently ready to mate now. Why else would those malicious bucks be trying to kill each other!"

Dark clouds gathered above the crown branch of the Great Pine. Horace shivered. The fur on his back stiffened. Ever since Zephyros told him Father had been killed, the sky frightened him.

"I'll get right to the point," Sylvester scowled at the blackening clouds. "Two hundred and seventy-two squirrel tails due east of here, lying in grass near a blackberry thicket, is a bevy of beautiful does. I heard them gossiping while I was making my calculations. They're crazy about you, Ecaroh. You dispatched the most brutal buck in the warren. You'll have your pick of the lot!"

The ladybug took flight. Beating her black-dotted red wings, she made three loops and landed on Horace's whiskers.

Horace sneezed.

"May you live a thousand moons!" Sylvester cried.

Horace sneezed again.

"And have a thousand children!"

Horace's eyes drooped. Ever so briefly—no more than a gust or two of wind—he slept.

"Perhaps," Sylvester flicked his tail seductively, "I'm being too discreet. As my father, a debonair and flirtatious gentleman, used to say, 'why call a crab apple an acorn?' You're not a child anymore; you're a full-grown lagomorph. Go home, find a wife, settle down, raise a family. Don't worry. Those dastardly bucks won't lay a whisker on you—not after the way you cracked that oaf's head. And if they do…" he punched the air with a balled-up paw.

A blast of wind tumbled from Mother Nature's weather pouch. The Great Pine groaned. A clump of green needles, loosed from its mooring, landed next to the root hollow.

Sylvester's ears twitched. He looked nervously at the darkening sky. Tail billowing, he leaped from the Great Pine. Hitting the ground full stride, he disappeared into the brush.

CHAPTER 22

Turbulent during the storm, Great Meadow air grew still and calm. Wind slept in Mother Nature's weather pouch. Pine needles stopped fluttering. The trunk of the Great Pine ceased to groan. A blackberry moon, bursting with pride, crept steadily across the luminous sky.

Horace foraged at the edge of the Great Pine's shadow. He ate miner's lettuce, chickweed, Queen Anne's lace, and vetch. Warm rain dusted his coat. When his belly was fully sated, he went back to the Great Pine and walked around the trunk. He circled three times in one direction and three times in the opposite direction—the way Mother taught him. After receiving the Great Pine's blessing, he followed a deer run through the lower swale. Moss cushioned his injured leg.

The Merry Little Breezes, frolicking and playing tag across the banks of the Lesser Stream, brought the scent of babbling water to the Great Meadow. Delicate and subtle, the scent reminded Horace of Meandra. He thought about her pink snout and shiny black eyes. He thought about the way she chewed blackberry bark, put the pulp in her paws then back in her mouth again. Had horsetail ferns fattened her up even more, he wondered? Had her tunnels stopped caving in? Was she spending more time on the meadow bank or the forest bank? When she greeted him after he crossed the Lesser Stream, she looked happy and plump.

Now a new scent reached Horace. But unlike the other scents Mother Nature uses to adorn her creations, this one didn't travel on wind. It couldn't. It wasn't place or thing. It wasn't earth or sky. It couldn't be touched or seen, heard or smelled. This is the scent one knows in a dream. Or when remembering something pleasant from the past. Or when looking forward to something pleasant in the future. This is the scent that makes newly hatched birds want to fly before their feathers are fully formed, the scent that makes fish swim upstream and hummingbirds come back to the same place after wintering thousands of miles away. The scent Mother Nature sent Horace made his fur stand out from his skin and his heart quicken. It made him feel like he could bound so high he'd never touch earth again.

Horace came to the place where the bog path splits, one run going to the Lesser Stream, the other to the blackberry thicket and the warren. Ears turning, nose quivering, he paused near a stand of towering teasel. He thought about cloud creatures and the sound of dragonfly wings. He thought about the taste of buttercup dew and the smell of twilight. He thought about Mother—her voice, the feel of her tongue, how she pulled fur from her chest to make his pillow.

Limping, Horace turned and started for home.

Epilogue

THE TWO-LEGGEDS CROSSED ON ROCKS THAT ROSE ABOVE the slow-moving water. From the Lesser Stream to the Ancient Bog they followed a deer run. From the Ancient Bog to the downed log they blazed a trail through towering teasel and low-lying yerba buena.

On one side of the downed log was meadow grass, on the other side a thicket of ripe blackberries. A pair of thrushes, purple berry juice dripping from their beaks, fluttered from bush to bush. The air was warm and still. A bumblebee, listing from a weighty load of pollen, flew past. Ants chewed pieces of rotted bark. Fluffy cloud-creatures drifted across the sky. The woman saw a cloud-bear. The man saw a cloud-muskrat.

When the two-leggeds reached the Great Pine, they ate pemmican and huckleberries. The woman gathered pine needles and wove a basket. The man took out a piece of obsidian and carved on the Great Pine's trunk. He carved his initials and those of the woman. Between their initials he carved a heart.

Horace discovered the marks when he was showing his son the root hollow. He had him lick the gathering pitch and explained that two-leggeds gnawed trees when they were mating. He told him about Sylvester, how he taught elocution to a toad and saved the Great Forest by getting moles and groundhogs to dig a trench the Great Fire couldn't cross.

At the end of summer, after the first big rain, yew saplings sprang up on both banks of the Lesser Stream—the first yews since lightning killed the Sacred Yew and Mother Nature separated hares and cottontails. A water vole said she'd seen a squirrel planting seeds. A badger said he'd seen Mother Nature pull saplings from her weather pouch. It also was rumored that two yews, one on each bank, were growing toward each other and would one day form a bridge between the Great Meadow and the Great Forest.

All that Horace told his son.

Fin

SVEVO BROOKS IS THE AUTHOR OF *THE ART OF GOOD LIVING* (Houghton Mifflin). A former elementary school teacher and professional athlete, Brooks volunteers in a large urban park and is a passionate advocate for public open spaces.

ILLUSTRATOR ZOE MENDEZ LIVES IN PORTLAND, OREGON with her family of humans and hounds. When not painting, Ms. Mendez tends to a pallet of radiant flowers and vegetables with her ducks following closely behind.

CPSIA information can be obtained
at www.ICGtesting.com
Printed in the USA
LVHW090917011221
703726LV00008B/10/J

9 781643 886954